This Book Belongs To:

Becky Conners
from her Great Grandma.
Christmas, 1982.

The Rand McNally Book of
Favorite Fairy Tales

RAND McNALLY & COMPANY Ⓐ **Chicago**

Established 1856

CONTENTS

Sleeping Beauty

ONCE UPON A TIME there lived a King and Queen
who had long wished for a child. And when one
day a sweet daughter was born to them the King
was so happy that he gave a great christening

feast. As godmothers for his little daughter he asked the seven good fairies in the kingdom. The one bad-tempered fairy was not invited.

After the christening there was a splendid feast. Before each fairy was placed an emerald plate, like a clover leaf, set with diamond dewdrops. Suddenly the .one uninvited fairy rode into the hall on a dragonfly, muttering threats.

Now the fairies, as was their custom, began to give their gifts to the Princess. The youngest gave her beauty; the next wit; the third, grace; the fourth, virtue; the fifth, a lovely voice; the sixth, a smile to win all hearts.

Then the uninvited, bad-tempered fairy cried out, "The King's daughter in her rosebud youth shall prick her hand with a spindle, and fall down dead!"

Everybody started to cry out, but then the seventh fairy popped up from behind the cradle and said, "Be comforted, O King and Queen! My gift is still to come. I cannot undo entirely what this unkind fairy has done.

"Your daughter will prick her hand with the spindle, but instead of dying she will sink into a deep sleep which will last a hundred years. From that sleep, when her dream is over, a king's son shall waken her."

Yet the King hoped to save his dear child from the threatened evil. He had his heralds proclaim that no one in all the country should have a spindle in the house.

One day when the Princess was fifteen years old, she went roaming about the palace, exploring one room after another. At last she came to a little room at the top of the tower. There an old woman sat busily spinning, as she had never heard of the King's proclamation.

"Good day, Granny!" said the Princess. "What are you doing?"

"I am spinning, my pretty lass," said the old woman. "Would you like to try it?"

"Oh, yes," the Princess cried. But when she caught at the whirling spindle it pricked her hand. She fell back in a faint.

The old woman, greatly alarmed, cried for help. People came running from all sides.

The King and Queen knew at once the fairy's evil wish had been fulfilled. They had the Princess carried to a room deep in the heart of the palace, and laid on a bed decked with green and gold covers. The King sadly commanded that she be left to sleep in peace until the hour of her awakening had come to pass.

Now the wise fairy, whose quick wit had saved the life of the Princess, knew what had happened and came at once in her swan chariot. She touched with her wand everything and everybody about the palace, except the King and the Queen. She touched the governesses and the ladies

in waiting, the gentlemen, the officers, the stewards, cooks, guards, and pages.

As she touched them, they all fell asleep, not to waken until their mistress should wake, and need them to attend her.

The King and Queen kissed their daughter, and left the hushed palace. The King issued a new proclamation, forbidding anyone to approach its gates. But such laws were not needed, for

soon a hedge of thorny shrubs grew around the palace grounds. They became so thick and high that neither beast nor man could force a way through. The castle itself was hidden. Only the top of the tower could be seen from a distance.

On the day that the hundred years ended, the son of the king then reigning was a-hunting and spied the tower beyond the forest. He asked what it was. An old peasant told him the legend of the sleeping princess and of the king's son who was to waken her. From the way the Prince's heart began beating, he felt certain that the peasant spoke the truth. He knew that he was the king's son who was to waken the princess. He set out at once. The great trees and thorns opened of their own accord to let him pass. And at last the castle stood before him.

He entered the courtyard and saw men and animals in deep slumber. The Prince crossed the court and mounted the stairs.

On he went to the very heart of the palace where, in a beautiful room of gold, he saw the loveliest sight in the world—a sleeping princess,

so fair she seemed an angel. He fell on his knees beside her and kissed her lovely cheek.

The Princess opened her eyes, smiled and said, "Is it you, my Prince? I have waited long."

They talked for hours and still had not said half that was in their hearts to say. Meanwhile,

everything in the palace waked with the Princess, and everyone took up his task just where he had left it. At nightfall a lady in waiting curtsied to the Princess and announced the wedding feast. Then the king's son led his bride to the royal chapel, where they were married.

The next morning the bridegroom and bride

left the palace and passed through the dark forest into the bright sunshine of the world beyond. And when the Princess turned to look at the castle where she had slept so many years, *behold*, castle and forest had vanished.

So the Princess rode with her Prince to his father's court, and there they lived a life as happy as her dream.

The Ugly Duckling

IT WAS SUMMER and lovely out in the country! In the midst of the sunshine lay an old farm surrounded by deep canals. Near the water a mother duck was sitting on her nest waiting for her ducklings to hatch.

One eggshell after another cracked open and little creatures stuck out their heads. But the biggest egg was still unbroken. When it did hatch, a large and ugly creature tumbled out.

"That is a terribly large Duckling!" said the Mother Duck. "None of the others look like that."

The next day the weather was fine. Mother Duck came down to the water's edge with all her little ones. Splash! into the water she jumped. "Quack! Quack!" she called, and then one Duck-

ling after another tumbled in. The water closed over their heads, but they came up in an instant, and floated beautifully. The ugly gray Duckling swam about with them.

"Quack! Quack! Come with me," said Mother Duck. "I'll take you out into the world, and introduce you to the duck yard."

But the other ducks in the yard looked at them, and said loudly, "Now we're to have all that crowd, too. There are enough of us already! And look at that ugly Duckling. We won't stand for him!" And one duck flew up and bit him in the neck.

"Let him alone," said Mother Duck. "He does no harm to anyone. He is good-mannered and swims as well as any of you."

But the poor Duckling that had been the last to hatch out and looked so ugly, was still being bitten and pushed around by the ducks.

He was in despair and decided to run away. He went over the hedge fence, and made the little birds in the bushes flutter up in fear. "That is because I am so ugly!" he thought.

He kept running on, and came to the great moor where the wild ducks lived. Here he lay all night, weary and downcast. In the morning the wild ducks flew up, and looked at their new companion.

"Pray, who are you?" they asked, and the Duckling turned in every direction and bowed as well as he could. "You are remarkably ugly!" said the wild ducks.

Again he ran away—traveling over field and meadow, and floating down the waterways.

Toward evening the Duckling came to a little hut, in which lived an old woman with her Cat and her Hen. The strange Duckling was noticed at once, and the Cat began to purr and the Hen to cluck.

"Who is there?" called the woman, looking all around. She could not see well, and she thought the Duckling was a fat duck that had strayed. "This is a rare prize," she said. "Now I shall have duck eggs."

The Duckling remained at the hut. But after a time, when he failed to lay eggs, the old woman ignored him.

This made the Duckling feel sad. He thought of the canal and was seized with a longing to float on it. He left the hut and swam on the water and was happy, but not for long. Other ducks always slighted him because of his ugliness.

The autumn came and the leaves in the wood turned yellow and brown. One evening, when the sun was setting, the Duckling saw a great flock of handsome birds. They were dazzling white, with long necks. They were swans. They uttered a peculiar cry, spread out their great wings, and flew away. They mounted so very high!

The Ugly Duckling had such a strange feeling as he watched them. He had never seen anything so beautiful. He turned round and round in the water like a wheel, stretched out his neck toward them, and uttered a strange, loud cry.

It would be too sad to mention all the misery
the Ugly Duckling had to go through during the
cold winter. He was so alone in the world!

He was lying out on the moor among the reeds
when the sun began to warm again and the larks
to sing. Beautiful spring had come.

All at once the Duckling raised his wings. They flapped with much greater strength than before and bore him swiftly away. Before he knew where he was, he found himself in a lovely garden, where the fragrant lilacs bent their long green

branches down to the winding streams. From the thicket came three glorious white swans. They ruffled their feathers and swam lightly on the water. The Duckling knew the splendid creatures, and he was overcome by a strange sadness.

"I will fly to them, the royal birds, and they will kill me, because I, who am so ugly, dare approach them. But it is better to be killed by them than to suffer so much misery."

He flew into the water and swam toward the beautiful swans.

"Kill me!" said the poor creature, and he bowed his head toward the water, expecting nothing but death. But what did he see in the clear water? He saw his own image and he was no longer a clumsy bird. He, too, was a swan! The great swans swam round him and stroked him with their bills.

Some little children came into the garden. The youngest cried, "There is a new one!"

The other children shouted with joy, "Yes, a new swan has arrived! And he is the most beautiful of all—so young and handsome!"

The new swan felt quite bashful, and hid his head under his wing, for he did not know what

to think. He was very happy, but not at all proud, for a good heart is never proud. He thought of how he had been scorned. And now he heard the children saying that he was the most beautiful of all beautiful birds! Then he rustled his feathers, lifted his slender neck, and cried joyously,

"I never dreamt of such happiness when I was still the Ugly Duckling!"

The Princess and the Pea

THERE WAS once a prince, who wanted a princess, but he would have nothing but a *real* princess. So he traveled all over the world to find such a princess. But no matter where he went there was always something wrong. There were plenty of princesses, but that they

were *real* princesses he could never be perfectly sure. There was always something or other that was not quite right. So at last he returned home, very downhearted, because he would have liked so much to have had a real princess.

One evening it was very stormy. The lightning flashed and the thunder crashed, while the rain poured down. It was really terrible weather! Then a knocking was heard at the outer gate of the castle and the old king went out to open it.

It was a princess who stood outside. But gracious, how she looked from the rain and the storm! The water streamed out of her hair and her clothes, it ran in at the toes of her shoes and out at the heels, and then she declared that she was a real princess.

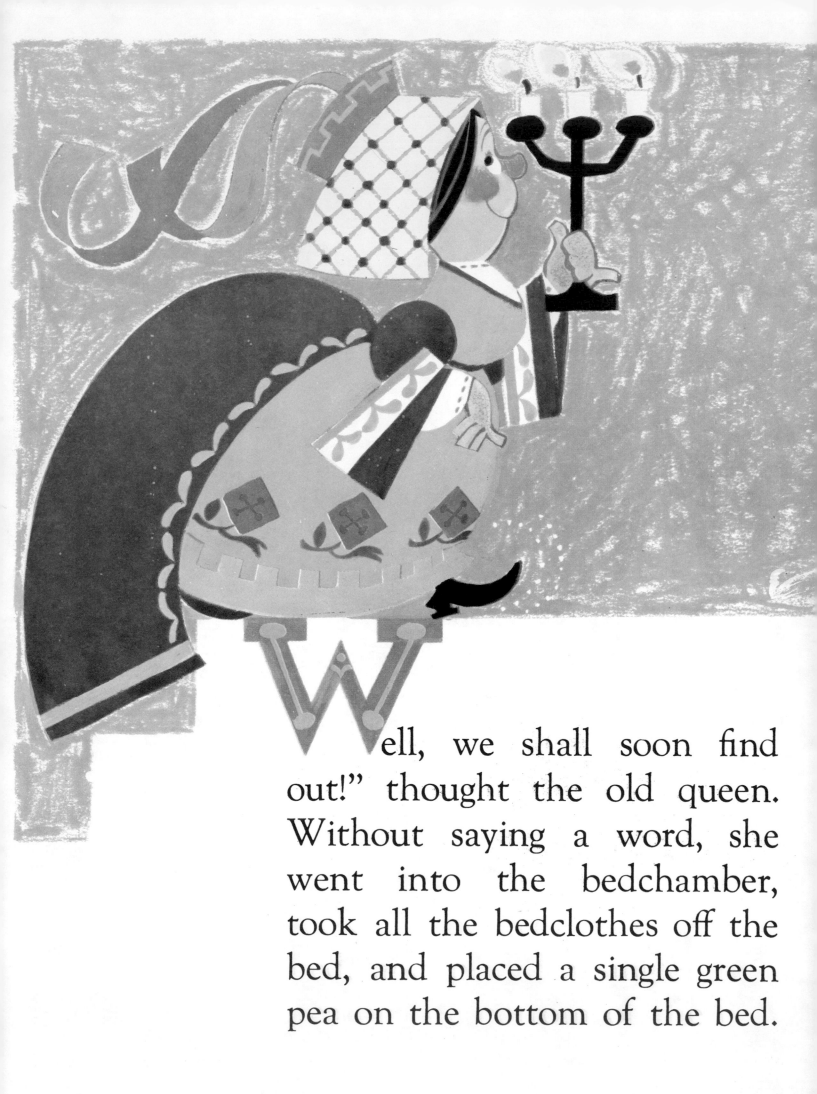

Well, we shall soon find out!" thought the old queen. Without saying a word, she went into the bedchamber, took all the bedclothes off the bed, and placed a single green pea on the bottom of the bed.

Then she took twenty mat-
tresses and piled them one on
top of the other over the pea,
and then piled twenty feather
beds on top of the mattresses.

THERE THE PRINCESS WAS
TO SLEEP THAT NIGHT!

In the morning they asked her how she had slept.

"Oh, wretchedly!" said the princess. "I have hardly closed my eyes all night long! Heaven knows what was in that bed! I have been lying on some hard thing, so that my whole body is black and blue with bruises! It is really terrible!"

Then they saw at once that she was a real princess, for she had felt the pea through twenty mattresses and twenty feather beds. None but a real princess could have so tender a skin and be so easily bruised.

So the prince took her to be his wife, for now he knew he had found a real princess. The pea was placed in the museum of art, where it may still be seen if no one has carried it away.

There, now I have told you a real story!

THE END

Rumpelstiltskin

ONCE THERE WAS a poor miller who had a beautiful daughter of whom he was very proud. One day he foolishly told the King his daughter could spin gold out of straw. The King loved gold above everything else, and he commanded that the maiden be brought to the castle.

When she arrived she was led to a large room half-full of straw. She was placed before a spinning wheel. The King said to her, "If all this straw is not spun into gold by morning, you shall die." He went out, and locked the door behind him with a huge key.

The poor girl sat down in a corner of the room and began to cry. She knew that she could not spin straw into gold.

Suddenly the door opened just a crack and a strange little man squeezed into the room.

"Good day, miller's daughter," he said. "What are you crying about?"

"Ah, me!" she sobbed, "I must die on the morrow, for I know not how to spin this heap of straw into gold."

"What will you give me if I spin it for you?" asked the little man.

"This necklace I am wearing," replied the maiden.

The little man agreed and, sitting down at
the wheel, spun it around merrily—*whirr, whirr,
whirr.* By morning the straw was gone and in its
place was the gold. Then he twisted the necklace
twice around his waist, and left as silently as he
had come in.

When the King came next morning, he was pleased to see the gold, but he wanted more. He led the girl to a larger room, two-thirds full of straw, and ordered her to spin it all into gold before sunrise.

And again the maiden began to cry, and again the little man slipped through the crack of the door and said, "What will you give me, miller's daughter, to spin your straw into gold?" "This ring on my finger," she replied.

So the droll little man set the wheel whirring again, twice as fast as before, and by daylight the straw was all spun into gold. Then he put on the ring and was gone.

The King came at dawn and was delighted to see the store of gold, yet his greedy heart was not satisfied. He took the miller's daughter into a vast chamber packed to the ceiling with straw. "Spin all this straw into gold this night," he said, "and tomorrow you shall be my queen."

As soon as the maid was alone, the queer little man appeared again and said to her, "Now what shall I have this time for my labor?"

"I have nothing more to give you," sighed the maiden.

"Then promise me your first child after you become queen," said the little man.

The maiden knew no other way out of her trouble, and promised to do what was asked.

That night the wheel whirred thrice as fast as before, and when the sun shone into the chamber, all the straw was gold.

The King was delighted to find all the straw spun into gold and, as he had promised, that very day he made the miller's daughter his queen.

At the birth of her first child the Queen was overjoyed. She had quite forgotten the queer little man until the day he slipped into her chamber and said, "Where is the child you promised me for spinning the King's straw into gold?"

The Queen wept bitterly and begged him not to take her baby. At last his odd little heart softened and he said, "I will give you three days to guess my name. If you can do it, you may keep the child." Then he slipped out of the room as quickly as he had come in.

The next day when the little man came, the Queen gave him the names of all the kings and princes that she could think of. But to all of them he gleefully answered, "Ho, ho! No, no, my Royal Dame! That's not my name! That's not my name!"

The next day the Queen sent messengers throughout the kingdom to collect all the curious names of poor folk. And when the little man skipped in, she began with Cow-ribs, Bandy-legs, Spindle-shanks, Snub-nose, and so on. But to all of them the little man shouted, "That's not my name!"

The third day the last of the messengers came back and said, "Forgive me, sorrowful Queen. I could find no new name but one. Yesterday, as I was passing through a strange wood, where foxes and hares say good-night to each other, I saw a small hut and in the doorway a funny little man sang this song,

" 'Today I bake, tomorrow I brew,
Today for one, tomorrow for two.
For how should she learn, poor Royal Dame,
That Rumpelstiltskin is my name?' "

When the Queen heard this, she knew the singer must have been her little gold-spinner.

At sunset the little man came skipping in and said, "Tell me my name if you can."

"Is it Hans?" she teased.

"No."

"Well, then, can it be Rumpelstiltskin?"

"The fairies have told you! The fairies have told you!" shrieked the little man in a rage, and he stamped his right foot so deep down through the floor that he could not pull it out. Becoming more angry still, he laid hold of his left foot with both hands and jerked so hard that he split himself in two, for he was really made of gingerbread, as are all Rumpelstiltskins.

Hansel and Gretel

ONCE UPON A TIME there lived near a large forest
a poor woodcutter with his wife and two children
by a former marriage—Hansel and Gretel.

The family had little to eat, and one night
the poor woodcutter said to his wife, "What will

become of us? How can we feed our children when we no longer have anything to eat even for ourselves?"

"I will tell you," she answered. "Early in the morning we will give the children some bread and lead them deep into the forest. Then we will go to our work. They cannot find their way home, and we shall be freed from them."

"No, wife," replied the poor woodcutter, "that I can never do." But the woman left him no peace until he agreed.

The two children had not gone to sleep, and they overheard what their parents said.

Hansel comforted Gretel, who wept bitterly. As soon as their parents fell asleep, he slipped outdoors and filled his pockets with the white pebbles which lay about, glittering in the moonlight. Then, going back to bed, he said to Gretel, "Sleep in peace, dear sister. God will take care of us."

Early next morning the wife awoke the two children. "Get up, you lazy things. We are going into the forest to chop wood. Here is a piece of bread for your dinner. You will get nothing else."

When they had gone a little way, Hansel stood still and dropped a pebble out of his pocket. This he did several times along the way.

When they were deep in the forest the children gathered wood and the father made them a fire. Then the wife said, "Now, children, rest yourselves while we go and chop wood. Later, I will come and fetch you."

Hansel and Gretel sat down by the fire, and fell asleep. When they awoke, it was dark. Gretel cried, "How shall we get out of the woods?"

But Hansel said, "We shall wait till the moon rises, and then we shall find the way."

When the moon came up, Hansel and his sister followed the pebbles, which glittered like new silver pieces and led them safely home. Their father was glad to see them, but the step-mother again planned to get rid of them.

Not long afterward the children overheard their stepmother saying to their father, "We have only half a loaf left. The children must go. This time we will take them still deeper into the woods."

As soon as their parents went to sleep Hansel got up, intending to pick up some pebbles as

before, but the wife had locked the door so that he could not get out. Still, he comforted Gretel, saying, "Do not cry. God will take care of us."

Early in the morning the stepmother pulled them out of bed, and gave them each a slice of bread.

On the way to the forest Hansel stopped every now and then and dropped a crumb upon the path.

The stepmother led the children deep into the woods, and said to them, "Rest here. We are going to a different part of the forest to chop wood. Later, I will come and fetch you."

When noon came, Gretel shared her bread with Hansel. Then they went to sleep. In the dark night they awoke. "We shall wait until the moon comes out," Hansel said to Gretel. "Then we can see the crumbs of bread, and they will show us the way home." But they could not see any crumbs, for the birds had eaten them all.

They walked the whole night and all the next morning. At last, the children heard a beautiful snow-white bird singing so sweetly that they followed it. It led the way to a cottage made of bread and cakes, with windowpanes of clear sugar candy.

"What a feast we shall have!" said Hansel. And he reached up and tore off a piece from the eaves, while Gretel broke off a peppermint stick from the door.

Then a sweet voice called out, "Tip-tap, tip-tap, who raps at my door?"

The children answered, "The wind, the wind, the child of heaven." And they went on eating.

Suddenly the door opened, and an old woman came out. Hansel and Gretel were very frightened. But the old woman said pleasantly, "Ah, you dear children—how hungry you must be! Come into my cottage. I shall make supper for you."

After a good meal of milk and pancakes, Hansel and Gretel lay down on two nice beds, and thought themselves in heaven.

Now the old woman was really a wicked witch who had built the bread and candy house to lure children to her.

Next morning, before Hansel and Gretel awoke, she leaned over them and mumbled, "That will be a good bite!" Then she shook them awake.

She locked Hansel in a little cage. "Fetch some water," she said to Gretel, "to cook something good for your brother who must stay in that cage until he is fat enough for me to eat." Gretel cried, but she had to do as the witch said.

Every morning the old witch said to Hansel, "Stretch out your finger!" But Hansel would stretch out a bone. The old witch, who could not see very well, thought it was his finger, and wondered why it did not get fat.

When four weeks had passed, and Hansel still kept thin, she would not wait any longer.

"Gretel," she called out angrily, "get some water quickly. Be Hansel fat or lean, today I will cook him."

The tears ran down Gretel's cheeks as she fetched the water. "Dear, good God, help us now!" she sighed.

"First we will bake," said the witch. "I have already heated the oven and kneaded the dough." So saying, she pushed Gretel up to the oven.

"Creep in," said the witch, "and see if it is hot enough for the bread."

Gretel said, "How shall I get in?"

"You silly girl," said the witch, "the opening is big enough. See, I could even get in myself!" She put her head into the oven. Gretel pushed her all the way in and shut the iron door. Oh, how horribly the old witch howled!

Gretel ran to Hansel, and opening his cage called, "Come out, Hansel, we are saved! The old witch is locked in the oven forever!"

And now, as there was nothing to fear, they went about the house, and filled their pockets

with the witch's secret treasure. Then they set
off, and after walking for hours they came at last
to a well-known part of the woods. When they
saw their father's house, they began to run. Burst-
ing into the kitchen, they fell into their father's
arms.

The poor woodcutter had not had one happy hour since he had left the children in the forest. His misery had gone from bad to worse. And in the meantime his wife had died of her evil disposition.

Hansel and Gretel gave the treasure to their father and forgave him. . . . So their sorrows came to an end, and they lived together in great happiness.